Young Sammy
El joven Sammy

Young Animal Pride Series
Serie: Jóvenes Animales Distinguidos

Book 9
Libro 9

Cataloging-in-Publication Data

Sargent, Dave, 1941–
    Young sammy = El joven sammy /
by Dave and Pat Sargent ; illustrated by
Elaine Woodward.—Prairie Grove, AR :
Ozark Publishing, c2006.
    p. cm. (Young animal pride series ; 9)

    "I'm a little stinker"—Cover.
    SUMMARY: An ornery little
skunk sprays everything in sight, until he
sprays Barney the Bear Killer. Barney
chases Sammy who promises to be good.
    ISBN 1-59381-239-6 (hc)
          1-59381-240-X (pbk)
          1-59381-241-8 (pfb)

    1. Skunks—Juvenile fiction. [1. Skunks—
Fiction.] I. Sargent, Pat, 1936– II. Woodward,
Elaine, 1956– ill. III. Title. IV. Series.

    PZ10.3.S243Sa 2006
    [Fic]—dc21   2003095973

Young Sammy
El joven Sammy

Young Animal Pride Series
Serie: Jóvenes Animales Distinguidos

Book 9   Libro 9

by Dave and Pat Sargent

Illustrated by Elaine Woodward

Ozark Publishing, Inc.
P. O. Box 228
Prairie Grove, AR 72753

Dave and Pat Sargent, authors of the extremely popular Animal Pride Series, visit schools all over the United States, free of charge. If you would like to have Dave and Pat visit your school, please ask your librarian to call 1-800-321-5671.

Foreword

Sammy is a little white skunk who loves to spray his stinky scent everywhere. He meets his match when he sprays Farmer John's dog, Barney the Bear Killer.

Prefacio

Sammy es un pequeño zorrillo blanco a quien le encanta rociar su apestoso aroma por todos lados. Se encuentra con "alguien de su tamaño" cuando rocía a Barney Mata Osos, el perro del granjero John.

My name is Sammy.

Mi nombre es Sammy.

I am a white skunk.

Soy un zorrillo blanco.

I smell bad.

Huelo mal.

I can stink!

¡Puedo ser muy apestoso!

I raise my tail.

Levanto mi cola.

I spray a cow.

Rocío una vaca.

I spray a dog.

Rocío un perro.

The dog is Barney.

El perro es Barney.

Barney chases me.

Barney me persigue.

I hide in a log.

Me escondo en un tronco.

Barney finds me.

Barney me encuentra.

He barks and growls.

Ladra y gruñe.

Better be good, Sammy.

Más te vale ser bueno, Sammy.

That is what he said.

Es lo que me dijo.

I nodded my head.

Asentí con la cabeza.

I will try to be good.

Voy a tratar de ser bueno.

I do not smell bad!

¡No huelo mal!

I smell like a rose!

¡Huelo como una rosa!

Oh, yeah!

¡Oh, sí!